Copyright © 2002 by Nord-Süd Verlag AG, Gossau Zürich, Switzerland
First published in Switzerland under the title *Tony auf dem Land*.
English translation © 2002 by North-South Books Inc., New York

All rights reserved. No part of this book may be reproduced or
utilized in any form or by any means, electronic or mechanical,
including photocopying, recording, or any information storage
and retrieval system, without permission in writing from the publisher.

First published in the United States, Great Britain, Canada,
Australia, and New Zealand in 2002 by North-South Books,
an imprint of Nord-Süd Verlag AG, Gossau Zürich, Switzerland.

Distributed in the United States by North-South Books Inc., New York.

Library of Congress Cataloging-in-Publication Data is available.
A CIP catalogue record for this book is available from The British Library.
ISBN 0-7358-1684-0 (trade edition) 10 9 8 7 6 5 4 3 2 1
ISBN 0-7358-1685-9 (library edition) 10 9 8 7 6 5 4 3 2 1
Printed in Italy

For more information about our books, and the authors and artists
who create them, visit our web site: www.northsouth.com

THE VISIT

By Fulvio Testa

Translated by Marianne Martens

North-South Books

New York / London

One beautiful summer's day, Mark, Emma, and Louis were hiking across the fields.

When they reached the highway, they saw a boy who was waiting at the bus stop.

"Hi, I'm Tony," he said.

"The next bus isn't until this afternoon," said Louis. "Why don't you come with us?"

So Tony went with them. But first he had to change his shoes.

"Tony, please turn the music off," said Mark. "Then you can hear the birds singing."

After a while they came to a pond.
Louis showed how good he was at
throwing stones. Mark played with
Tony's electronic game.

Later, Mark, Louis, and Tony explored an abandoned house while Emma picked flowers.

Mark shook apples down from an apple tree and shared them with everyone.

Tony took his sunglasses off and looked at his apple. "It looks just like the apples in the supermarket," he said, "but it tastes much sweeter!"

The dog ran ahead and scared a cow.
Tony stood at the fence and watched.

"A cow! A real live cow!" Tony was amazed. He had never seen a real live cow before.

As they crossed over the next hill, they heard a bus. It was time to say good-bye.

"I'll never forget this day," said Tony.
"We won't either, Tony," said Mark,
Emma, and Louis.

Tony rode the bus back to the city. What a great day! he thought. Those kids shared so much with me. He didn't realize that he had shared a lot with them, too.

Mark, Emma, and Louis stood at the highway and thought, Tony shared so much with us! But they didn't realize how much they had shared with him.